D1384505

NORMAN BRIDWELL
Clifford's®
SPRING CLEAN-UP

SCHOLASTIC INC.

New York   Toronto   London   Auckland   Sydney
Mexico City   New Delhi   Hong Kong   Buenos Aires

For the next generation:
Alison's Sophie, Michael, Beatrice, and Raphael;
Ashley's Alexander and Emma Rose;
Caroline's Sam;
Emily's Alissa;
and Melissa's Henry and Natalie

ISBN-13: 978-0-590-06012-7
ISBN-10: 0-590-06012-0

Copyright © 1997 by Norman Bridwell.

12 11 10 9 8 7 6 5 4 3   8 9 10 11 12/0

Printed in the U.S.A.   23
First Scholastic printing, April 1997

Happy spring! I'm Emily Elizabeth.

At our house, it's time for spring cleaning again.

Last year, the whole family worked hard—

even my big red dog, Clifford.

My first job was to hang some rugs out to air.

Clifford wanted to help.

He took a rug outside and gave it a good shaking.

I guess he shook it a little too hard.

Mom said we might as well wax the living room floor

as long as the rug was up.

Mommy and Daddy started to move the furniture outside.

When Clifford saw the couch, his eyes lit up.

He used to curl up on it when he was a small puppy.

CRUNCH!

He didn't fit on it anymore.

Good thing the couch was so old.
Daddy was going to get a new one anyway.

There was still a lot of spring cleaning to do.

Clifford cleaned the windows all by himself.

First he washed them . . .

. . . then he dried them.

Mommy didn't think Clifford's method worked very well.

So we washed the windows again.

Poor Daddy. He had to rake the yard.
It looked as if it would take him all day.

But not with Clifford to help!

Just then some of my friends came by.

They asked me to help them clean up the vacant lot
on the corner. It was their Earth Day project.

Clifford did his part for Earth Day.

Then we planted a beautiful garden.

On the way home, Clifford and I saw some people
working on another Earth Day project.

Clifford gave them a hand . . .
er, a tail.

Back at home, there was another job to do.
Clifford's house needed some spring cleaning, too.

He swept out his old bones . . .

. . . and tossed out his collection of rubber toys.

It made quite a large pile.

Somehow Clifford got it all into the garbage truck —

much to the surprise of the driver.

Now both our houses were neat and clean.

It was a good day's work.

About Earth Day

On April 22, we celebrate Earth Day.

It's a time to do something special for your neighborhood.

Clean up a yard or sidewalk, plant some flowers, write a poem or sing a song about the wonderful plants and animals Nature has given us.

Make every day Earth Day.